SECRETS OF THE LIBRARY OF DOOM

EXPRESS

THE GHOST RIDDLE

BY MICHAEL DAHL
ILLUSTRATED BY PATRICIO CLAREY

T0372125

raintree

a Capstone company — publishers for children

Raintree is an imprint of Capstone Global Library Limited, a company
incorporated in England and Wales having its registered office at 264
Banbury Road, Oxford, OX2 7DY – Registered company number: 6695582

www.raintree.co.uk
myorders@raintree.co.uk

Text © Capstone Global Library Limited 2024
The moral rights of the proprietor have been asserted.

Designed by Hilary Wacholz
Original illustrations © Capstone Global Library Limited 2024
Originated by Capstone Global Library Ltd
Printed and bound in India

978 1 3982 5355 1

British Library Cataloguing in Publication Data
A full catalogue record for this book is available from the British Library.

CONTENTS

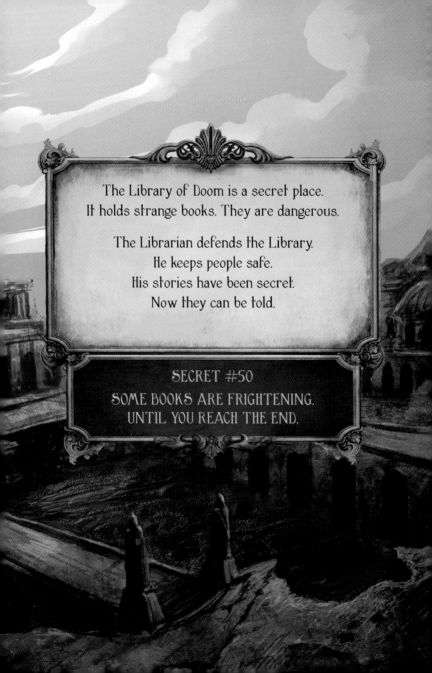

The Library of Doom is a secret place.
It holds strange books. They are dangerous.

The Librarian defends the Library.
He keeps people safe.
His stories have been secret.
Now they can be told.

SECRET #50
SOME BOOKS ARE FRIGHTENING.
UNTIL YOU REACH THE END.

Chapter One

HOUSE ON THE HILL

"It's a **STORMY** night!"
says Sam.

"Perfect for ghost stories," says Jill.

The girls are driving down a road.
They are going to Jill's aunt's house.

It is raining.
The road is very **MUDDY**.

Thunder rumbles.

RRRRRUUUMMMMMM!

"My aunt likes ghost stories," says Sam.
"She liked one called *The Three Whistles*.
It had a creepy riddle."

Lightning FLASHES.

The girls see an **OLD** house.
It is on a hill.
There is a big gate.

"Is that your aunt's house?" asks Jill.

"Yes," says Sam. "But why is it so dark?"

Chapter Two

THE OPEN WINDOW

Sam parks the car.

It is still raining.

The girls **RUN** to the house.

The front door is open.

The girls step in.

A door upstairs slams shut.

"Aunt Carrie!" yells Sam.

She **RUNS** upstairs.
Jill follows.
Sam opens a door.

"This is my aunt's bedroom," she says.

The girls walk in.
The room has many shelves.
There is **NO ONE** there.

The window is open.
The wind blows in.

There is a book by the window.

It is open.

On the book is a whistle.

It is **OLD** and silver.

Jill picks up the whistle.

"No!" **SHOUTS** Sam.

Chapter Three

THE WHISTLER

Jill blows into the whistle.

TWEEEEE!

Sam grabs the whistle.
She **THROWS** it out of the window.

"Why did you do that?" asks Jill.

"The whistle!" says Sam. "It's like the one in the story. The GHOST story!"

A green light FLASHES outside.

"The light is coming from the graveyard," says Sam.

Jill is pale.

"What is going on?" she asks.

"In the story, there are three whistles," Sam says. "Each whistle brings something **HORRIBLE**."

CRASH!

The girls look out.
The gate is **SMASHED**.
A figure is in the garden.
It is green.
It GLOWS!

Suddenly, it disappears.

"Where did it go?" asks Sam.

They hear the front door.
It smashes open.

Jill shouts, "It's in the house!"

Chapter Four

THE THING

Sam locks the bedroom door.
They hear heavy footsteps.

"We must hurry," says a voice.

The girls look behind them.
There is a shape in the corner.
It looks like a woman.
Her face is hidden.
The girls can see through her!

"It's a ghost!" cries Sam.

CRUNCH! CRUNCH!

The footsteps are coming.

"I can help you," says the ghost. "But you must hurry."

The ghost moves to the window.
She points to the BOOK.

"We MUST have the whistle!" says
the ghost.

"It's in the garden. I threw it," says Sam.

TAP-TAP-TAP-TAP

They look at the other window.
Someone is tapping there.

Jill **SCREAMS**.

A man is out there.
He is FLOATING.

Chapter Five

THE RIDDLE

"Don't let him in!" yells Sam.

"It's all right. Trust us," says the GHOST.

The window opens.

The man **CLIMBS** in.

He wears a long coat.
He has **DARK** glasses.
He is holding the whistle.

Then . . . the door handle begins to turn.

"Now!" **SHOUTS** the ghost.

The man blows the whistle.

TWEEEEEEEE!!

The house **SHAKES**.
A green light flashes.
Then everything is **SILENT**.

"The **GRAVEYARD** ghoul is gone,"
says the man.

The GHOST is gone too.
A woman stands there.

"Aunt Carrie!" says Sam.
"But how?"

"Remember the **RIDDLE** in the story?" Aunt Carrie asks.

Sam nods and says,

"The first brings the GHOST.
The second brings the **GRAVE**.
The third brings the END."

"I found the book," says Aunt Carrie. "There was a whistle on it. I had a strange feeling. I *had* to use it."

"The first turned you into a ghost," says Sam.

"Then mine called the thing from the grave," says Jill.

"Then the third brought the end," says the man.

The man picks up the book.

He picks up the whistle.

He nods to Aunt Carrie.

Then he **FLIES** out of the window.

"Aunt Carrie!" gasps Sam. "Who was that?"

"That was my old friend," says Aunt Carrie. "That was the LIBRARIAN."